Who's Asleep?

Who's asleep in their bed?

npp

NorthParadePublishing

Who's asleep in the nest?

Who's asleep in
the shell?

Mother
Blackbird and
her chicks!

Who's asleep in the cave?

Who's asleep
in the barn?

It is Brian the bear!

It is Clarence
the cow!

Who's asleep
in the basket?

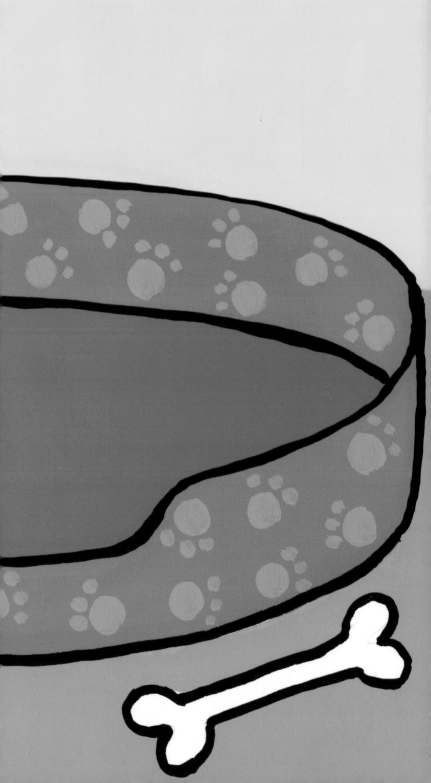

It's Doug the dog!

Who's asleep
in the hutch?

It's Fluffy the bunny!

Who's asleep
in the bed?

It's YOU and ME!

Herman the crab!

Now everyone
is asleep!

written and illustrated by Emily Bolam